Fierce Milly

and the

Amazing Dog

D0755830

Also by Marilyn McLaughlin:

Fierce Milly

Winner of the Bisto Eilís Dillon Award

and a Bisto Merit Award

Fierce Milly

and the
Amazing Dog

Marilyn McLaughlin

Illustrated by Leonie Shearing

mammoth

To Jack, Lassie, Dusty, Dinah, Rory, Whisky, Murphy, Shandy, Ruby, Oscar, Tessie and Jodie
MML

In memory of Gareth
LS

First published in Great Britain in 2001
by Mammoth, an imprint of Egmont Children's Books Limited,
a division of Egmont Holding Limited,
239 Kensington High Street, London W8 6SA

Text copyright © 2001 Marilyn McLaughlin
Illustrations copyright © 2001 Leonie Shearing

The moral rights of the author and illustrator have been asserted.

ISBN 0 7497 4239 9

3 5 7 9 10 8 6 4 2

A CIP catalogue record for this book
is available from the British Library

Printed in Great Britain
by Cox & Wyman Ltd, Reading, Berkshire

Contents

1. Fierce Milly's new dog

Fierce Milly was practising going down our street superfast on her bike. Me and Billy had to time her with Billy's birthday watch. She did something terrible. She put her arms up in the air and took her feet off the pedals, so that they whirred round all by themselves. She whizzed down the street, shouting, 'No hands! No feet!' It was nearly no Fierce Milly, because she forgot about stopping at the end of the street. She swerved across the road, bashed into the kerb, flew through the air, bounced off Mrs McMichael who was coming out of the corner shop, and fell in a pile in the middle of all the groceries that Mrs McMichael had dropped.

There was flour and broken eggs everywhere. 'It's like when she's making pancakes,' Billy said.

Mrs McMichael was saying, 'Oh dear me, oh dear me,' and Fierce Milly was roaring louder than she had ever roared

before. But her bike was all right.

Everybody ran out into the street. Tony from the corner shop said, 'Not a lot wrong with her if she can yell that loud.'

Then Fierce Milly's mum came running up and said she'd take Fierce Milly to hospital for a check-up. We could still hear Fierce Milly roaring, long after the car had gone round the corner.

It was very quiet in our street with no

Fierce Milly there. There was nothing to do. Me and Billy went up the street and down the street, slowly, to make it last longer. Nothing happened. The dogs came out and snoozed on the doorsteps. The cats lay down on the tops of the garden walls. The birds came down and pecked at things in the gutters. Nothing loud happened, nothing sudden happened. We went home to see if lunch was ready. It was. It was sausages and beans. That was OK.

When we went out again we were really glad to see the car back outside Fierce Milly's house.

'Race you,' said Billy and off he went.

Fierce Milly must have seen us coming because she had the door open before we could ring the doorbell.

'My mum's still cross about the superfast bike-riding,' she said. 'I'm not allowed out to play and I'm not allowed to ride my bike.

And I hurt my arm, really sore.'

'Did your arm come right off?' Billy asked. 'Like with Susan's Barbie?'

'It came right off,' Fierce Milly said. 'And they put it back the wrong way round so my elbow worked backwards and they had to take it off and put it on again, just like changing light bulbs.'

'That's only a story, Billy,' I said, just in case he believed it.

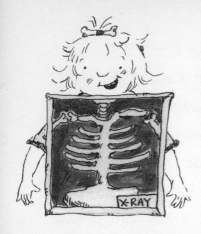

'And they did an X-ray and I got to see all my insides,' Fierce Milly said.

'That might be true,' I said.

'Yeuch,' said Billy.

Then Fierce Milly's mum came and said that if she was feeling well enough she had to go and say sorry to Mrs McMichael.

'Wash your face first,' she said, but she was too late, for Fierce Milly was already away, the garden gate still swinging open behind her. Fierce Milly was always in too much of a rush for face-washing and gate-shutting and hair-combing and coat-buttoning and toilet-flushing and all that sort of thing.

'I wanted her to take these flowers and groceries,' Fierce Milly's mum said. 'Will you take them after her, Susan, and make sure she remembers to say sorry.'

I took the groceries because of the eggs, and Billy took the flowers. When we caught up with Fierce Milly she was already at McMichaels' front door and she was shouting in through the letterbox, 'Woof, woof, woof,' and something inside was barking back, even more loudly, 'WOOF! WOOF! WOOF!'

'It's a wolf,' Fierce Milly said.

'When did McMichaels get a wolf?' Billy asked.

Then a door opened inside and the barking got louder.

'It's a pack of wolves,' Fierce Milly said.

Then we could hear Mrs McMichael saying, 'Down Rover,' in a wolf-commanding sort of voice and the front door began to

open. Billy dropped the flowers and hid behind me. I hid behind Fierce Milly. It wasn't a wolf. I knew it wouldn't be a wolf. It was a tiny little round white fluffy dog, jumping up and down like a demented yo-yo on fast forward, barking its head off. The more Mrs McMichael said, 'Down, Rover,' the more Rover bounced and barked.

So she picked him up and tucked him in tight under her elbow, which meant that Rover McMichael came face to face with

Fierce Milly. It wasn't a particularly nice face, because there was lunch on it. There was mashed potato and gravy and jam and custard and chocolate. But Rover didn't mind. He sniffed. He smiled. Fierce Milly smiled back. This was her first time to see a dog close up. They always run away from her, because she is so sudden and loud. Then Rover tried to lick Fierce Milly's tasty face, but Mrs McMichael swung him away just in time.

'He likes me,' she said. And everyone could tell that she liked him. If she had a tail she would have wagged it. Mrs McMichael was very pleased with the flowers even if they were bruised from Billy dropping them, and she was very pleased with the groceries.

 'What a sweet girl to think of that,' she said, and patted Fierce Milly's head.

'What sort of dog is Rover?' the sweet girl asked.

'A poodle,' said Mrs McMichael.

Billy clapped his hand over his mouth and went all red. I made a be quiet face at him.

'Where do you get dogs from?' Fierce Milly asked.

'You'd have to talk to your mother about that,' Mrs McMichael said.

'Right,' said Fierce Milly, and off she went.

'She forgot to say sorry,' I said. 'She was supposed to say sorry for crashing into you.'

'That's all right,' Mrs McMichael said. 'I know she's sorry.'

Well, I wouldn't have known she was sorry, but then grown-ups have all sorts of strange ways of knowing things. So we said goodbye to Rover McMichael and goodbye to Mrs McMichael and went after Fierce Milly. Billy was ready to burst.

'Poodle,' he said and then started chanting. 'Poo-dill, Pee-dill, Poo-dill.'

He did it all the way to Fierce Milly's house. When we got there, she was sitting on the doorstep looking sad.

'My mum says I can't have a dog. She says I can't even look after myself so how would I look after a dog? She says I can't have a dog until I'm sensible.'

'No dog then,' Billy said. 'You'll never be sensible.'

We sat down beside her, because we could imagine how sad it is, not to have a dog, when you want one.

'You've still got us,' Billy said. And then he had a bright idea. 'I'll be your dog. Except at bedtimes and dinner-time.'

'But I want an all-the-time dog,'

Fierce Milly said, and then she had a bright idea. 'And I know how.'

She went into the house and after a while came back with an old dog-collar and lead. 'It belonged to my dad's favourite dog when he was wee, and now it belongs to my dog, Crazy Eyes.'

'Where is he then?' I asked.

'On the lead,' Fierce Milly said. 'He's very big with huge teeth. He's a very rare mouse-hunting poodle.'

'I don't see any Poo-dill,' Billy said.

'Shut up, Billy,' I said. 'It's not funny.'

'Not everyone can see this type of dog,' Fierce Milly said. 'That's what's so rare about them, and why they're so good at hunting mice. The mice can't see them at all.'

Billy was just about to say something that would make trouble when Fierce Milly said, 'And anyone who laughs at my dog will grow a tail.' Billy's mouth shut again quickly and he put his two hands behind him to check, just in case.

That night he drew a Happy New Dog card for Fierce Milly. He drew her on it and just an empty space for Crazy Eyes. 'Seeing as nobody knows what he looks like.'

'At least she's happy again,' I said. 'Even if we do have to put up with smelly old Crazy Eyes.'

'Is he smelly, Susan? Did you smell him? How can you smell a dog you can't see? Is

he really there, Susan? Can just Fierce Milly see him and just you smell him? Does he bark, Susan? If he eats something does it go invisible inside him or would you see just a sausage walking about, or does he have to eat invisible food? Does Crazy Eyes do invisible poos?'

'Shut up, Billy.'

2. Fierce Milly vanishes

Billy and me were playing at the bottom of our garden. Billy was digging a hole, big enough to get in.

'Why don't you stop, Billy? It's big enough now,' I said.

'I want it to be big enough for you to get in too, Susan.'

'We could take turns getting in it, first you, then me.'

'It's not the same. I want us to be both in it together. Then no one will see us.

We can be spies.'

Then a strange noise came from the street. Clip clop clip clop clip clop. It was getting closer and closer.

'I never heard a noise like that before,' Billy said. 'Is it a baby dinosaur with a wooden leg?'

I'm older than him, so I knew what it was.

'It's Fierce Milly wearing her mother's high heels,' I said.

bread

We looked out over the garden gate and it was Fierce Milly, coming our way. She wasn't just wearing her mother's high heels. She was wearing her mother's best party frock too. On

Fierce Milly it went down to the ground and she had to hold it up with one hand. She had a great big fat handbag in the other hand. She was saying over and over again, 'Eggs and sugar and bread, eggs and sugar and bread, eggs and sugar and bread.' So we knew she was going to the corner shop.

'Where's Crazy Eyes?' Billy asked, because Fierce Milly usually has her invisible dog Crazy Eyes with her.

'He is in the bag because I don't have any hands spare to hold the lead. Eggs and sugar and bread. Eggs and sugar . . .'

'Won't he eat the shopping on the way back, if he's in the bag?' Billy asked.

'He would do,' Fierce Milly said. 'Eggs and sugar and bread. I know what I'll do.'

She put the bag on the ground, got the collar and lead out and tied Crazy Eyes to the lamppost just outside our garden.

 'Eggs and sugar and bread. Keep an eye

on him until I get back. Sometimes he howls when I leave him. Eggs and sugar and bread, eggs and sugar and bread . . .' and off she went.

Crazy Eyes was very quiet. He didn't howl. He didn't move. Watching the lead on the lamppost got very boring, so me and Billy went back into the garden to dig at the hole.

Then Cecil Nutt and Joe came along. Joe is sometimes our friend. Cecil Nutt is never our friend. He stopped outside our garden to make fun of Crazy Eyes' lead.

'What's this old lead doing here? Why, it's Fierce Milly's stupid old dog, all on its ownio. I'll just take it for a walk.' And he took the lead off the lamppost and ran away fast. By the time me and Billy got out

of the garden Cecil Nutt and Joe and Crazy
Eyes were gone.

'He took Crazy Eyes. That's not fair.'
Billy was nearly crying.

'He's only a pretend dog. He won't mind.'

'I mind and Fierce Milly will mind.'

Fierce Milly did mind. When she came
back and there was no Crazy Eyes she
jumped right out of her mother's high heels
and jumped up and down on the pavement
yelling, 'Dognapper! I'll put him in the

blender, I'll put him down a volcano, I'll iron him flat with the steam iron . . .'

Then we heard Cecil Nutt's whoop coming from round the corner.

'He's coming back,' I said.

'Are you going to be violent?' Billy asked, his eyes all big and round.

'Not in high heels, not in bare feet,' Fierce Milly said and she ran into our garden, threw the handbag into Billy's hole and jumped in after it, party frock and all. The high heels were left standing, side by side on the pavement, pointing up the street towards Cecil Nutt who had just turned the corner. Joe was still with him, and Cecil Nutt was swinging the lead round in the air.

Fierce Milly hissed out of the hole just behind the hedge, 'Don't let on I'm here. Act bored.'

So me and Billy stood at our garden gate,

acting bored. Billy tried to whistle, but it was only pretend whistling, and the closer Cecil Nutt and Joe came, the tinier the whistling got, because Billy is scared of Cecil Nutt. By the time they reached our gate Billy's whistle had shrunk all away. We just stood there silent, hoping we looked bored.

The two high heels stood in the middle of the pavement, blocking the way. A huge voice roared out, 'You give my dog back!'

It was Fierce Milly at full volume. We all jumped. Then me and Billy tried to look bored again.

'Where are you?' asked Cecil Nutt.

'Right here in front of you. Don't you see me shoes?' roared Fierce Milly from the hole. 'The rest of me's invisible.'

'It's a trick. You're hiding on us,' Joe said, and the two of them ran all around, looking for Fierce Milly. They looked under the parked cars. They looked in next door's gardens

22

both sides and they looked in our garden, but they didn't see Fierce Milly in the hole. Cecil Nutt looked up all the lampposts. Joe looked down the gratings. Then they stood around, trying to look bored and unimpressed. Me and Billy didn't bother looking bored any more. This was good.

'How did you do that then?' Cecil Nutt

asked the shoes on the pavement. 'How did you go invisible?'

'It's just something I found out how to do the other day. I can do it any time and I can go about invisible for days and days. I sneak up behind people and do terrible things to them. Do you want me to come back again?'

'Yes.'

'Then give my dog back.'

'OK, here's your stupid dog then,' and he held out the lead.

'And stop calling it names.'

'OK, here's your nice dog,' and he held the lead out again.

'Well, my hands are full, aren't they? Give it to Susan.'

So I got to hold Crazy Eyes' lead. It felt just like an ordinary lead and it didn't do any of the jumping about that it does when Fierce Milly holds it. Crazy Eyes was so well-behaved you wouldn't know he was there.

'He likes you,' Billy whispered.

Then Fierce Milly said that she was ready to come back. She said that we all had to stand with our backs to her and close our eyes tight and that if anybody peeped their eyes would fall out.

'I want to see it happen,' Cecil Nutt said.

'No, you don't,' Fierce Milly said. 'I come back from the inside out, bones first, then the gooey bits and then my skin and then my clothes and my eyeballs last.'

'Yeuch,' said Cecil Nutt and Joe and they

turned round right away. So did Billy. Maybe he'd forgotten it was just a trick.

'Make Crazy Eyes turn round too, Susan. He might run off with one of my bones. Now nobody turn round until I tell you.'

I could feel Fierce Milly in her bare feet tiptoe out through the garden gate just behind me. I knew she'd get in the shoes and then just stand there. Cecil Nutt and Joe and Billy all had their eyes screwed up tight. But I was peeping.

'Here comes my liver,' said Fierce Milly behind us, 'and my guts and my blood.'

Billy put his fingers in his ears.

'Here come my kneecaps and my toes and my fingernails,' said Fierce Milly.

Billy pulled his jumper up over his head.

'Here comes my skin. Where's my tummy-button?

Oh, it's round the back. My skin is on back to front. I'll just have to do it all over again.'

'Hurry up, Fierce Milly,' I said. 'I need to go to the bathroom.'

'Well, why don't you just go?'

'I don't want to miss anything.'

'Oh all right then. You can look now.'

But nobody would turn round, only me.

'Is she all back to front?' Billy asked, and wouldn't look.

'See if I care,' Cecil Nutt said and he turned round. 'Aw, she's just ordinary.'

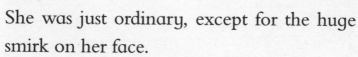

Then Joe and our Billy had a look. She was just ordinary, except for the huge smirk on her face.

'Now, go away you and don't come near Crazy Eyes again, or I'll go invisible and do terrible things.'

'See if I care,' Cecil Nutt said again. 'It's all some stupid old trick anyway.' But you could see that he wasn't sure. 'Come on, Joe, let's go and do something *sensible*.' And Cecil Nutt never bothered us again, for days and days and days.

But Fierce Milly's mum bothered her.

'Broken eggs in my handbag? What is it with you and eggs? And mud on my best frock! When will you ever learn to be sensible?'

3. Fierce Milly and the magic spell

Fierce Milly said that she had a pet slug called Slither. She said that he was the fastest slug in the street. She said that he went all the way up the back of her house and in her bedroom window and he only took three days.

'How do you know it was the same slug? It might have been a different slug that was there already,' I said. I was fed up with always having to be impressed by everything Fierce Milly did and everything she said.

'I'd know my own slug anywhere. It was my Slither all right.'

'Have you two pets now?' Billy asked. 'Slither as well as Crazy Eyes? Does your mum allow you two pets?'

'Well, she doesn't know about Slither,' Fierce Milly said.

'Do you keep a slug in your bedroom? Yeuch,' I said.

'Well, I don't any more. That's why I'm sad today,' Fierce Milly said. 'Crazy Eyes ate Slither.'

'No!' said Billy.

'Good riddance to Slither,' I said.

'I didn't know Crazy Eyes was in the room. I let Slither out of his jam jar, just so he could go for a slide on the windowsill, and when I looked back again he was gone. Stop laughing, Susan. It's not funny.'

'It's because of Crazy Eyes being invisible,' Billy said. 'It could have happened to anyone's slug. Let's have a funeral for Slither. It'll cheer you up.' Billy's always having funerals, even for things that aren't really dead, like an empty matchbox, like a broken plate.

'Well, I'm going for a nice little walk,' I said. 'With my doll's pram, in my new plastic sandals. Are you coming?'

'No,' Billy and Fierce Milly said together.

'Huh! Go on then, bury your old slug that isn't even there any more, because it got eaten by a rotten invisible dog that no one can see. Huh! I bet your old Crazy Eyes isn't really there at all. He's just makey-uppy and doesn't exist.'

Fierce Milly went pale and fierce. 'He's my dog and he's there if I say so.'

'Prove it.'

'OK then. I will. Just you wait and see,' and she stormed off.

'Come on, Billy,' I said. 'You come and

be the baby in the pram and I'll push you up and down the street.'

But he wouldn't get in the pram. He went up the street after Fierce Milly. That wasn't fair because he's my little brother and he's supposed to do what I say.

So I just walked up and down the street with the pram. I didn't want to go to some old slug's funeral. But it was boring going up and down the street with just the pram and nobody with me. Then Billy came back, but he went right on past me and up our garden. I shouted after him, 'What are you doing?'

'It's a secret,' he shouted back and went into the house. I went on pushing the pram, up and down, up and down, keeping an eye out. Billy came back out of the house.

'Where are you going?' I asked.

'Not saying,' he said and away he went, off up the street without me. So I set off after him, pram and all. If he looked back and saw me, I'd just pretend I was pram-pushing, not following. He went round the corner, up past the houses, past the park gate and down the back lane, right to the yellow door that belongs to Fierce Milly's backyard. He knocked and Fierce Milly came out. They both had secret things hidden up their jumpers.

I pushed the pram down the lane, slowly, slowly, so that they wouldn't notice it getting closer and closer and I stayed ducked down

on my hunkers behind it, so that they wouldn't see me. And they didn't either. They never knew I was there. Just as I sneaked right up beside them and could hear what they were saying, Billy shouted out, 'Hey Susan!' He can never keep a secret. 'Fierce Milly's making a magic spell to make Crazy Eyes visible. It's real magic too.'

I was so surprised I forgot about not being

34

seen and popped up from behind the pram.

'How do you know how to do magic?' I asked.

'Tell your big sister I'm not speaking to her,' Fierce Milly said to Billy. 'And tell your big sister that I know how to do it because I'm making it up. If I can make up Crazy Eyes, I can make up dog-appearing magic too.'

They made a pretend fire with a ring of stones filled with grass from the edges of the lane. They put on dandelion heads and a snail-shell, and a black feather Fierce Milly found. She said it was a dragon's feather. Then she walked round and round the fire making gurgling noises and terrible faces. It looked good. I wished I was doing it too, but if she wasn't speaking to me, I wasn't speaking to her.

'Spider bones,' Fierce Milly said, and Billy took out the black plastic spider he got last

Christmas. Then there was a terrible whoop from the far end of the lane. It was Cecil Nutt, coming our way.

'Oh no,' said Billy. 'He'll wreck our spell. He'll kick it to bits. He'll jump on it with his big boots. He'll break the magic.'

'It might get loose. It might go anywhere,' Fierce Milly said.

'Loose magic!' Billy's eyes got big. 'It might get into me!'

'Get out of here!' Fierce Milly yelled.

'I've a better idea,' I said. Nobody wants to leave a laneway full of loose magic. I pushed the doll's pram over the top of the magic fire. You wouldn't know it was there. Cecil Nutt didn't see it at all.

'What are you lot doing then?' he asked.

Fierce Milly always knew how to get rid of Cecil Nutt.

'We're playing at walking about with the pram,' she said. 'You can play too. You can be the daddy.'

'No way,' Cecil Nutt said and he ran off fast.

When I wheeled the pram back off the magic fire everything was still where it should be.

'Great,' said Fierce Milly. 'Come on, Susan. Now for the last bit.'

She was speaking to me again, so I got to be part of the spell after all. She got out a bottle of hand-cream. She said it was magic potion, but I know it was hand-cream because my mum has one the same. I didn't say, in case it spoiled the magic. We all put cream on our hands and then we had to hold hands and dance round the fire. That was difficult because we kept coming apart because of the slippy hand cream. Then Fierce Milly said some magic words, 'Yzarc seye emoc evila.' Then we all stood around waiting to see if the magic worked. Nothing happened.

'How long does it take?' I asked.

'I don't know. I never did magic before,' Fierce Milly said.

So we waited a wee while longer. Still nothing happened.

'Let's try some more magic words,' Fierce Milly said. 'Maybe he just didn't hear us.'

Fierce Milly climbed right up on top of her backyard wall and shouted really loudly.

'Yzarc seye emoc evila.
WHERE ARE YOU?'

Billy climbed up on
the doll's pram and he
started shouting
as loud as he
could, 'Crazy
Eyes, WHERE
ARE YOU?'

So I climbed up on top of the bin and I
yelled for Crazy Eyes at the top of my voice
too. It was great. Then the yellow door burst
open and an absolutely huge voice roared,
'MILDRED!'

'It's a talking dog,' shouted Billy.

'It's my mum,' said Fierce Milly.

And it was, with her hands all soapy from
washing dishes. 'And what is all this noise
about? And what has happened my good
hand-cream?' The empty bottle was lying
on the ground on top of the magic fire.

'In, Mildred. Go and tidy your bedroom. That'll quieten you down.'

So me and Billy and the pram and the magic fire were left alone in the middle of the back lane.

'Did Crazy Eyes go in too?' Billy asked.

'How would I know?' I said.

But just then Fierce Milly opened her bedroom window. Tidying her bedroom hadn't made her any quieter yet.

'Good news,' she yelled.

'The spell worked?' Billy yelled back up.

'No. I just found my My Little Princess lunchbox that was lost under my bed, and guess what?'

'What?'

'Slither was hiding in it, just for a laugh.

He didn't get eaten after all.'

Then her mum yelled, 'MILDRED!' again, so she had to go.

'I don't want to be here any more,' Billy said, 'in case Crazy Eyes appears. I want to go home.'

So he hopped in the pram and we set off for home fast. On the way Billy said, 'Susan, if a slug was laughing in your My

Little Princess lunchbox, what would it sound like?'

'Yeuch, Billy. It would just sound yeuch.'

4. Fierce Milly and the bubble dog

Me and Billy went to call for Fierce Milly. There was a surprise on her doorstep. It was a dog! It was the smelliest, ugliest, biggest dog in the world. It lifted up its head and looked at us. It tried a sort of dog smile and its eyes rolled around in its head as if they were loose.

'It's Crazy Eyes! He's really here!' Billy said. 'The spell worked! Now everyone can see him.'

'Too bad that everyone can smell him!'

I said.

We held our noses and stepped over the dog to ring the doorbell.

'Do all poodles smell like that?' Billy asked.

'They don't even look like that,' I said.

It was very early in the morning and Fierce Milly was still in her pyjamas, so she wouldn't open the door. She opened the letterbox and peeped out.

'Is it still there?' she asked.

'Yes,' Billy said. 'Is it Crazy Eyes? Did the magic work?'

'It followed me home yesterday, and my mum won't let it in the house because it's so smelly. And she says that it's not my dog, and she wants it to go home. But I think it's Crazy Eyes. I want to keep it.'

I said, 'We'll give it a bath, and then maybe your mum will let you keep it.'

'OK,' Fierce Milly said. 'Wait for me to get dressed.'

'Your dog needs some breakfast,' Billy said.

The letterbox snapped shut.

The smelly dog sat up and me and Billy and it stared at the letterbox, waiting to see what would happen next. A bowl of chocolate cornflakes for the dog happened next. It ate it all up. And then there was one of those awful rude exploding noises and a terrible smell – the worst one ever.

'Fierce Milly!' me and Billy yelled, because it was usually her who did that sort of thing.

'It wasn't me,' she said,

and we all turned and stared at the dog.
It stared back at us, looking nearly sorry.
Its eyes sort of wobbled and rolled
around again, just as if they were about to
come out.

'Oh, it *is* Crazy Eyes,' Fierce Milly said. 'I
just know it. I'm going to keep him.'

Fierce Milly's mum was out and her dad
never notices anything so we sneaked Crazy
Eyes in the front door and up the stairs.

We all squeezed into the bathroom. It was a tight fit. Crazy Eyes was a big dog and did a lot of tail-wagging.

Fierce Milly ran the taps and dipped in her elbow to see if it was too hot or cold. 'That's the way you do it for babies,' she said. She knew all about babies because her auntie had a new one and sometimes she was allowed to help. But I bet her auntie usually rolled her sleeve up before testing the water.

Fierce Milly never noticed that she had a dripping sleeve. 'In you get,' she said to Crazy Eyes. But he wouldn't get in. We tried pushing and we tried putting bits of him in to give him the idea, and Fierce Milly tried her loud bossy voice. Nothing worked.

Then Fierce Milly had a brilliant idea: she put some chocolate cornflakes in the

bath. Crazy
Eyes knew what
those were, so he
hopped right in, SPLASH! and ate up the
floating cornflakes. Then he drank some
bath water and ate the soap.

'Soap's gone,' Billy said.

Fierce Milly opened up Crazy Eyes' huge
mouth and peered right down inside there.

'All gone, not a scrap left.'

Billy went round the back end of the dog.

'What are you doing, Billy?' I said.
'That's the really smelly end.'

'I know,' Billy said. 'I'm waiting for the
next you-know-what, to see if it comes out

in bubbles because of the soap.'

'Good idea,' Fierce Milly said. 'Keep an eye there, Billy, we wouldn't want to miss that.'

I said that they were both revolting, and they could wash their own horrible dog. I was going home. Nobody paid me any attention. So I stayed anyway, or I might have missed something. I would have missed the bubble mountain, which was the next thing that happened. And that happened because Fierce Milly decided to use her mum's refreshing aromatherapy bubble bath to wash Crazy Eyes.

'You have to add it to running water,' she said and she poured the whole lot in under the running taps.

'Look at that,' Billy said, because the bubbles grew and grew and grew. Crazy Eyes was disappearing under them, looking surprised. He took a big mouthful and licked his lips and took another one, but he wasn't eating the refreshing aromatherapy bath bubbles fast enough to stop them bulging up over the top of the bath.

'Turn the taps off!' I shouted.

Fierce Milly screwed her eyes up and leaned right into the bubble mountain. We could hear her hands going slap-slap-slap as she felt about for the taps and then we heard the water stop. But Crazy Eyes thought she was getting in the bath with him and he started wagging his tail and that made the bubbles fly up into the air. They floated round the room and stuck to the ceiling in big clumps.

Billy grabbed some and made himself a beard. He thought it was great, but Fierce Milly didn't.

'Stop that, Crazy Eyes. My mum doesn't allow splashing in the bath. We've got to get rid of the bubbles.'

'Pull the plug on the bath,' I yelled. So Fierce Milly did and all the water swooshed out of the bath, but it didn't take the bubbles with it. She began scooping them up and dumping them down the toilet, and when it was full up she tried to flush them away, but they just boiled up like a volcano. She shut the lid on the toilet and sat on it.

'It's a bubble emergency!' she yelled. 'Chuck them out the

window.' We climbed up on the toilet seat to open the window and threw great big armfuls of aromatherapy bubbles out into the backyard. The wind caught them and floated them away.

'Like big snow, like fat birds, like balloons,' said Billy.

Then Crazy Eyes shook himself and more bubbles and water flew all over the bathroom. We all got wet, the floor got wet, the toilet roll got wet and all the towels were wet.

'Do you think my mum will notice?' Fierce Milly asked.

'I think even your dad would notice,' I said.

'Do you think we should go for a long

long walk and maybe come back tomorrow? She might have forgotten about the wet bathroom by then.'

You never know how long grown-ups take to forget things. But a walk sounded like a good idea. We set off for the park. Crazy Eyes got a bit drier on the way, and at least now he smelt of refreshing aromatherapy stuff, which was a change. But he was still a very ugly dog.

'Are you sure you want to keep this dog?' I asked.

'I have to, if it's Crazy Eyes. I invented him and I made him visible.'

'Why couldn't you have made up a nice dog, like Rover McMichael?' Billy said.

'Well, I didn't know he was ugly like this when I made him up, did I?' Fierce Milly said.

Just then, just as we came into the park, Crazy Eyes put his nose up and sniffed the air. Then he ran away as fast as he could.

'Crazy Eyes, come back!' Fierce Milly shouted, 'I didn't mean it about you being so ugly. You're all right really. You just need getting used to.'

We went about all over the park shouting, 'Crazy Eyes, Crazy Eyes.' Then a bubble floated past Billy, and another one and another one.

'It's Crazy Eyes,' Billy yelled. 'He must be burping or something!' and we followed

the bubbles in round behind some bushes. Billy was really pleased. 'I was right. If you eat soap you burp bubbles.'

And there, round behind the bushes was Crazy Eyes, but he wasn't making bubbles. He was jumping about catching them, and a little old lady on a park bench was blowing them.

'Hello,' she said when she saw us. 'I knew my dog would find the bubbles. She's been lost, and I've been so sad without her. But bubble-chasing was always her favourite game. So I've been going about everywhere blowing bubbles and now she has found me again. Don't you ever run away again, you naughty, naughty Fiona.'

'*Fiona*!' said Fierce Milly on the way

home. 'To think I nearly had a dog called *Fiona*. No wonder she ran away from home.'

'Are you sad it's not Crazy Eyes?' I asked. 'Are you going to try the magic spell again?'

'Maybe, someday,' she said.

But she never did.

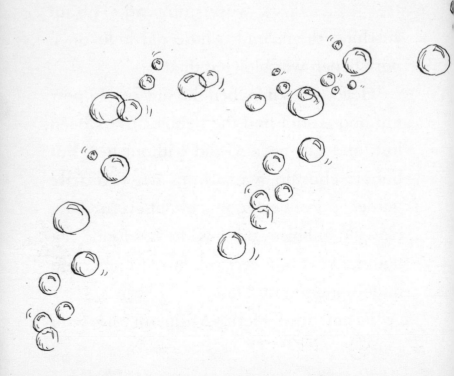

Be afraid. Be very afraid:
Fierce Milly is here!

Her yellow-hand monster sends fear through
the neighbourhood and her pet dinosaur runs amok.
Even the dogs and cats in the street run from her in alarm!

Only when she rescues Billy AND helps Susan
to fly, do they discover her heart of gold.

by Marilyn
McLaughlin

illustrated by
Leonie Shearing

The first Fierce Milly storybook